This Igloo book belongs to:

....

igloo

Published in 2011
by Igloo Books Ltd
Cottage Farm
Sywell
NN6 0BJ
www.igloo-books.com

M044 0111
10 9 8 7 6 5 4 3 2 1
ISBN 978-0-85734-518-9

Illustrated by: Simone Abel, Jackie East, Masumi Furukawa, Paige Billin-Frye,
Paula Knight, Kim Martin, Barbara Vagnozzi, Liza Woodruff
Original stories and re-tellings by: Laurence Burden, Gaby Goldsack, Patrice Lawrence,
Sue McMillan, Alison Morris, Louise Rooney, Linda Watters

Printed and manufactured in China

Stories
for
Girls

igloo

Contents

Stories for Younger Girls

Thumbelina . . . . pages 6-13

Little Red Hen . . . . pages 14-17

The Golden Goose. . . . . . . pages 18-27

Tha Magic Dancing Shoes . . . . pages 28-37

Chicken Little . . . . pages 38-41

Snowfall the Unicorn. . . . . . . pages 42-47

Stories for Older Girls

Snow White & Rose Red . . . . pages 48-55

The Missing Pony . . . . pages 56-63

The Bee Wing Ball Gown . . . . pages 64-71

The Six Swans . . . . pages 72-79

The Butterfly Garden . . . . pages 80-87

The Little Mermaid . . . . pages 88-96

Thumbelina

O nce there was a wife who longed for a little girl. So she went to see an old wise woman to ask for her help. "I wish for a little girl more than anything in the world," sighed the wife. "Won't you please help me?"

"With all my heart," replied the kindly old woman, and she gave the wife a barley seed. "This is not like the seed the farmer sows," said the old woman. "This is a special seed, which you must take home and plant in a pot."

The wife took the seed and planted it. Soon a beautiful yellow and red flower grew. The wife thought it so beautiful that she couldn't help kissing it. At once, the petals unfurled. There in the middle sat a delicate girl with golden hair. She was tiny, smaller even than a thumb, so the wife named her Thumbelina.

The wife and tiny girl were happy together. During the day, Thumbelina played on the table, singing songs in her sweet voice. At night, she slept soundly in a bed made from a walnut shell, with rose-petal blankets.

One night an ugly toad came hopping in through the window and saw Thumbelina asleep. "What a pretty wife she will make for my son," she said, and she picked up the bed, then hopped out of the window, down to the stream. She placed the bed on a water lily. "She cannot escape from here," thought the toad.

Thumbelina

When Thumbelina awoke and saw where she was she began to cry.

"Dry your tears," croaked the toad, swimming over. "You are to marry my son, and you shall live together down in the mud."

But the toad's son was very ugly. Poor Thumbelina did not want to marry him. "Who will save me now?" she sobbed.

Luckily, the fish in the stream felt sorry for the beautiful girl. When the toad was sleeping, they chewed the stem of the lily leaf on which Thumbelina sat. At once, the flowing water carried Thumbelina and the leaf off down stream, far way from the ugly toads.

She was just beginning to feel happy again, when suddenly a large beetle buzzed down, seized her and flew high into a tree. Finally, he put her down on a leaf.

"How pretty you are," the beetle told the tiny girl. "Would you like some honey?"

It wasn't long before the other lady beetles heard about the tiny girl, and came to see Thumbelina for themselves.

"She only has two legs. How ugly!" laughed one, giving Thumbelina a prod.

"Look! She has no feelers," cried another. "How odd!" Embarrassed by their laughter, the male beetle picked up the tiny girl and set her down on a daisy below.

All summer and autumn Thumbelina lived in the wood. She made a bed from grass, sheltered by a leaf. She ate nectar from the flowers, drank dew from the leaves and sang with the birds.

When winter arrived it grew very cold. The birds flew away, leaving Thumbelina alone. Her clothes were worn and she could find nothing to wrap around herself. She was also very hungry; she had to find food and shelter for the winter. She walked through the wood until she came to a hole where a field mouse lived. Thumbelina knocked on the door.

When the kindly mouse saw the little girl, she was filled with pity. "Come in, child," she said. "You must be frozen."

The mouse listened in silence as Thumbelina told her story. Then she smiled. "Why don't you come and live with me?" she suggested. "To repay me, you can help to clean my house, tell me stories and sing me songs."

So Thumbelina stayed with the mouse and did what she was asked. One day the mouse told Thumbelina that her friend the mole would be visiting. "He is most handsome," she said. "He would make you a fine husband."

When the mole arrived, he took quite a fancy to Thumbelina.
"This is a passage between my home and yours," he said, showing Thumbelina
a dark tunnel. "You are most welcome to use it to visit me anytime. But do be
careful. There is a dead bird in there."

Thumbelina looked into the tunnel. There on the floor lay a dead swallow.
When she saw the poor bird, tears filled her eyes. "I will bring him a cover,"
she whispered, stroking its feathers.

As Thumbelina placed the cover over the swallow, she was surprised to feel his heart
beating. The tiny girl was filled with joy. The bird was alive!

All through the long winter, Thumbelina cared for the swallow. Finally, when spring
arrived, Thumbelina knew her friend was strong enough to fly once more.
"It's time for you to leave," said Thumbelina bravely. Then she made a hole in the
roof of the tunnel, so the swallow could escape.

Thumbelina

"Why don't you come with me," said the swallow. But Thumbelina could not leave the mouse after all her kindness. So she gave the bird one last hug, then watched as her friend flew away.

That night, the mole asked Thumbelina to marry him. Although she did not want to, Thumbelina agreed, just to make the mouse happy.

Every evening the mole visited to talk about the wedding, as Thumbelina stitched her wedding clothes.
"My home is very snug," he would tell her. "No nasty bright sunlight at all."
Thumbelina's heart sank. The more she listened, the unhappier she felt. How could she possibly live without the sun?

Finally, the day came when the mole would fetch his wife and take her deep into his dark hole.

Thumbelina thought her heart might break.
"Goodbye sun," she cried. "Goodbye flowers."
And she kissed a nearby daisy.

Suddenly, there was a fluttering of wings. Thumbelina looked up to see her friend the swallow flying above. "Oh, Swallow," she cried, "today I must say goodbye to the sunshine forever." And she told him all about the mole and his dark, dark home. "Come with me," said the swallow. "It will be cold here again soon, but I am flying far away to a warm country, where the sun always shines."

"Yes, yes!" cried Thumbelina, climbing onto the swallow's back. "I could never make the mole happy. He should marry Mouse instead."

The swallow soared into the air, swooping over mountains and forests, until at last they came to a warm country, where the sun shone brightly. He came to rest near a lake, where a ruined palace covered in trailing vines rose up into the sky. "This is my home," said the swallow, placing Thumbelina gently on the petals of a flower.

Thumbelina

Thumbelina rubbed her eyes in amazement. There inside the flower sat a tiny young man no bigger than a thumb, with gossamer wings. As soon as she laid eyes on him, Thumbelina fell instantly in love.

"I am the King of the flower spirits," said the tiny man, gazing at the beautiful girl before him. Then he took off his crown and placed it gently upon Thumbelina's head. "Will you be my bride and become Queen of the flower spirits?" he asked. "With all my heart," replied Thumbelina, unable to believe how happy she felt.

At last, she had found her true home.

Little Red Hen

Little Red Hen was pecking and clucking in the farmyard when, all of a sudden, she came upon a grain of wheat.
"I could eat this wheat," she said to her friends, "or we could plant it in the ground and then maybe it will grow and feed us all."

And so she asked, "Who will help me plant this grain?"
"Not I," quacked the duck.
"Not I," honked the goose.
"Not I," mewed the cat.
"Very well," said Little Red Hen. "Then I shall plant the grain."
And so she made a little hole in a clearing and planted the grain all by herself.

The very next day, Little Red Hen looked at the spot where she had planted the grain and saw that it was dry. And so she asked her friends, "Who will help me water this grain?"

"Not I," quacked the duck.

"Not I," honked the goose.

"Not I," mewed the cat.

"Very well," said Little Red Hen. "Then I shall water the grain."

And so she brought a watering can and gave the grain a cool drink. And she did the same the next day, and the day after that, all by herself.

Very soon, the grain had grown into tall, ripe wheat, good enough to eat.

So Little Red Hen asked her friends, "Who will help me cut this wheat?"

"Not I," quacked the duck.

"Not I," honked the goose.

"Not I," mewed the cat.

"Very well," said Little Red Hen. "Then I shall cut the wheat."

And so she brought a scythe to cut the wheat and then she gathered it all up, all by herself.

Now the wheat was ready to be ground into flour, so she asked her friends,
"Who will help me take this wheat to the miller?"
"Not I," quacked the duck.
"Not I," honked the goose.
"Not I," mewed the cat.
"Very well," said Little Red Hen. "Then I shall take the wheat to the miller."

And so she put the wheat on the cart, and she drove the cart to the mill.
The miller saw that the wheat was very good indeed, and there was enough to make a whole sack of flour, which Little Red Hen took back to the farm all by herself.

Now the flour was ready to be baked into bread. So Little Red Hen asked her friends, "Who will help me bake the bread?"
"Not I," quacked the duck.
"Not I," honked the goose.
"Not I," mewed the cat.

"Very well," said Little Red Hen. "Then I shall bake the bread." And so she kneaded the dough and put it into the oven. When it smelled good and ready, she asked her friends, "Who will help me eat this bread?"

"I will," quacked the duck.

"I will," honked the goose.

"I will," mewed the cat.

"Hmmm," said Little Red Hen. "No one would help me plant the grain, water it, cut the wheat, take it to the miller or bake the flour into bread. But everyone will eat it?" she asked.

"Yes," quacked the duck.

"Yes," honked the goose.

"Yes," mewed the cat.

"I don't think so," said Little Red Hen, and she ate up the bread – all by herself.

The Golden Goose

Once upon a time, there were three brothers. The two older brothers were clever and strong, but the youngest was small and shy. The rest of the family teased him and called him names.

One day, their father told them he needed some wood from the forest for the fire. The oldest and strongest brother jumped up.

"Father, let me go," he said. "I am the strongest and the smartest. I will go into the forest and bring back more wood than you'll ever need!"

So his mother gave the brother a loaf of freshly baked bread and a bottle of good wine. "Take these," she told him. "You will need something to nourish you and quench your thirst."

When the oldest brother reached the forest, he met an old man.

"Good day to you, young sir," called the old man. "I am famished. Do you have any bread?"

"Yes," replied the brother, "but I need it for my own lunch. I cannot spare any."

"In that case," said the man, "do you have anything to drink? I have had nothing all day!"

"I'm sorry," said the brother. "I would give you some wine, but I need it for myself. Chopping wood is thirsty work. Now, if you don't mind, I'm very busy, so I must be on my way!"

"It is a shame you cannot spare anything for me. Remember this if something happens to you," replied the old man mysteriously.

The oldest brother marched off into the forest and found a fine tree to chop.
He had not been working long when CHIP! CHOP! OUCH! His hand slipped,
and the axe cut him.
"Oh! Oh! My poor finger!" he cried and ran home, wondering all the way if the
strange old man had something to do with the accident.

The next day, the second brother went to his father.
"Father," he said, "I feel it is my duty as your second-born son to take up the work
my poor injured brother could not finish yesterday." So he too was given a lunch of
fresh bread and wine, and off he went to the forest to chop wood.

When he reached the forest, the second brother met the same old man.

"Good day to you, young sir," smiled the old man. "Could you spare some
of your lunch for a hungry old man?"

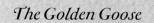

The second brother thought for a second. "I do have some bread," he replied, "but I surely cannot spare any, for I don't want to starve myself!" "Then maybe a little of your wine to ease my thirst?" asked the old man. "If you drink it, what shall I have when I am thirsty from chopping wood?" replied the second brother. "I'm sorry. You'll have to find some of your own. Now, if you will excuse me, I have work to do." "It is a shame you cannot spare anything for me. Remember this if something should happen to you," the old man replied.

With that, the brother marched off into the forest, and began work. CHIP! CHOP! OUCH! The axe slipped and struck him on the foot. He let out a howl and he cursed the strange little man, for he was sure that this accident was his doing. Then he hopped all the way home!

21

The Golden Goose

The next day, the youngest of the three brothers went to his father.
"Let me go to chop wood for the fire," he said. "My brothers are in no state to work, and so it falls to me to finish the job."

The older brothers mocked their younger sibling, and laughed that he would be too weak to chop the wood. But the family needed the wood, and so the youngest brother was sent on his way. There was no fresh bread left, and his older brothers had drunk all the wine, so all he was given was a piece of stale crust, and a flask of water from the well.

When the youngest brother reached the edge of the forest, he too met the little old man.
"Would you share your lunch with me?" the old man asked the boy.
"I only have stale old bread and water," replied the youngest brother, "but you are welcome to share it."

The old man thanked him. And when the boy took out the bread, it was as fresh as the morning it had been baked. What was more, the water had turned into sweet wine.

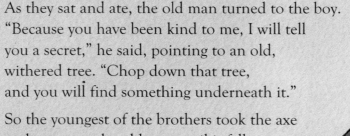

As they sat and ate, the old man turned to the boy.
"Because you have been kind to me, I will tell you a secret," he said, pointing to an old, withered tree. "Chop down that tree, and you will find something underneath it."

So the youngest of the brothers took the axe and swung at the old tree until it fell.

22

The Golden Goose

There, sitting among the roots, was a goose with feathers of pure gold.

The youngest brother knew that if he returned home, the goose would be taken away from him, so he found an inn where he could stay. The innkeeper had three daughters, and when they saw the goose, each one secretly decided they would wait for the right moment and then pluck one of the golden feathers.

Later that evening, when the boy was sleeping, the eldest of the daughters crept into his room and seized the goose. But when she tried to pull her hand away, she found that she could not remove a single feather. She was stuck fast!

Next came the second daughter, looking for a feather to pinch. But the very moment she touched her sister, she also became stuck!

The third sister came in soon after, and thought she had chanced upon a game the other girls were playing. She ran to her sisters, and before they had time to warn her, she too was completely stuck!

The Golden Goose

The next morning, the boy awoke to find the innkeeper's three daughters attached to the golden goose. To teach them a lesson, he picked up the goose and marched right out of the door, so that the daughters had to follow him wherever he decided to go.

As he marched them through the streets of the village, they passed the church. "Dear me," cried the priest, who was standing outside. "What a shameful thing it is to see three girls chasing some poor boy through our little village. Let go of him, I beg you." And he reached out to pull at the youngest daughter's sleeve as they passed by.

But as the priest grabbed hold of her, he too became stuck fast by the goose's magic, and so was forced to run behind them.

The Golden Goose

The youngest son led the procession out of the village and into the fields, where they passed two farmers.

When the priest saw these big, strong men, he called out to them. "Please help! I'm stuck! Perhaps the two of you could pull me free?"

So the farmers ran over and took hold of the priest. But as soon as they did so, they too became fixed and had to follow wherever they were led.

Soon the boy reached the city. The King who ruled the city had a beautiful daughter who was very sad. No one could cheer her up. In desperation, the King had put forth an order saying that any man who could make his daughter happy could have her hand in marriage.

As soon as the youngest of the brothers heard this, he went directly to the royal court, followed by the innkeeper's three daughters, the priest and the two farmers, of course.

When the King's daughter witnessed this strange procession, she immediately burst into peals of laughter! The King, however, did not like the look of this silly boy and his goose, and changed his mind about the promise he had made.
"You can only marry my daughter if you bring him a man who can eat a mountain of bread," he told him.

So the boy went back to the forest where he had first found the goose. There, he found the little old man, sitting on a tree stump, as before.
"I am so hungry, I could eat a mountain!" cried the old man, rubbing his tummy.
"Do you know where I can find more food?"
"I do," replied the boy. And he took the old man back to the royal court, where a huge mountain of bread had been baked. The old man ate and ate and ate.
By the end of the day the mountain was gone, and the old man had disappeared. Still the King was not satisfied.

The Golden Goose

"If you want to marry my daughter you must bring me a ship that can sail on land and water!" he demanded, certain this time that the boy would fail.

But the boy was wiser than he looked. "The old man has helped me twice," he thought to himself. "Why not a third time?"

So he returned to the forest to find the old man. Sure enough, he found him waiting in a clearing.

"Because you are kind and generous, I will help you one last time," said the old man. In a flash there was a huge ship with wheels and sails, standing right next to them!

The youngest brother climbed aboard and sailed the ship across fields and lakes, meadows and rivers, all the way back to the city.

When the King saw this, he couldn't believe his eyes. But he knew there was nothing he could do. Reluctantly, he agreed at last to the marriage.

And so the youngest son, who was once teased and made fun of, married a princess and became a royal prince. In time, the young couple inherited the kingdom. The brothers and parents of the youngest son begged his forgiveness for teasing him, and the son, being generous of heart, invited them to live in his kingdom. And so they all lived happily with each other for many years after.

The Magic Dancing Shoes

Annabel wanted nothing more than to be able to dance. Her grandmother had been a very famous dancer, and Annabel would spend hours looking at all the old photographs and trophies at her grandparents' house. She would imagine herself on stage, in the spotlight, dancing in front of a huge crowd.

But no matter how hard she tried, Annabel couldn't make her feet do what she wanted them to. She watched enviously as the other girls in her class twirled across the floor. "Why am I so clumsy?" she would sigh.

One day, Annabel was visiting her grandparents' house, when her grandma took her aside. "How are the dancing lessons going, Annabel?" she asked.
"Oh Nana, I just can't do it!" cried Annabel. "I'm always practicing, but I just can't get it right."
"Of course you can!" laughed her grandmother. "You just have to believe you can do it. Now wait there a moment. I have something for you."

Nana came back with a cardboard box and handed it to Annabel.
"Well, open it!" she laughed.

Inside the box, hidden beneath crumpled brown paper, was the prettiest, most delicate music box Annabel had ever seen. She opened it to find a little fairy ballerina spinning around to a simple, elegant melody.
"It's beautiful Nana! Thank you!" cried Annabel.

"It belonged to me when I was a little girl," said Nana. "You must promise to take very good care of it. That music box is much more special than you think."

Annabel wasn't really sure what she meant by this, but she gave her a big hug and then ran off to show her parents the wonderful gift.

29

When they got home, Annabel went straight up to her room and wound up the music box. She watched as the fairy ballerina twirled around and around.

"How I wish I could dance like you!" Annabel sighed. As she spoke, there was a flash. Before Annabel's startled eyes, the fairy ballerina in the box yawned, stretched her arms, then fluttered into the air, before coming to rest lightly on Annabel's bed.

"Thank you, Annabel," said the fairy ballerina in a tiny voice. "It feels so good to be out of that box at last! Now I would like to do something for you. When you wake up in the morning, you will find a pair of dancing shoes at the foot of your bed. Put them on and you shall become the greatest dancer in the world!"

The Magic Dancing Shoes

Without another word, the fairy flew into the air and out of the open window.
Annabel could hardly believe what she had seen.
"My imagination must be playing tricks on me," she thought, as she climbed into
bed that night. She knew that fairies didn't really exist. And as for a pair of magic
shoes that could make you dance – she had never heard such a ridiculous idea!

All night the little ballerina danced through Annabel's dreams. And when Annabel
woke up, she couldn't resist checking at the foot of her bed . . . even though she was
sure there would be nothing there.
But to her astonishment, she found a pair of beautiful dancing shoes,
just as the fairy ballerina had promised!

The shoes didn't look very magical, but Annabel couldn't wait to see if they would really work. She slipped them on her feet and stood in the middle of her room, ready to attempt a pirouette. Before she had a chance even to think about what she was doing, she found herself spinning around on the tips of her toes like a real ballerina. She could dance! Unable to believe it, Annabel tried the other steps she had learned in class. She performed them all perfectly.

"What will Miss Carr say?" she giggled, as she spun round and round.

Annabel's dance teacher, Miss Carr, was very impressed with her progress.
"You have been working hard, Annabel!" she said at the next class.
"Yes," replied Annabel, smiling to herself. "My nana helped me."

Later that term, Miss Carr took Annabel aside. "I think you are ready to take on one of the lead roles in the show at the end of term," she said.
"Would you like to?"
Annabel was overjoyed. "Oh yes!" she cried. "Thank you so much!"
Then she ran off to tell her mother and father the wonderful news.

The following week, Miss Carr announced the show in class. There were mutters of disapproval from some of the older girls when they found out Annabel had the lead role. But Annabel tried not to care what the others thought. She just wanted to dance! So she worked as hard as she could to learn all the new steps for the show. Of course, the magic shoes made it a lot easier – but Annabel still worked harder than ever before. She wanted every single step to be perfect.

Finally, the day of the show came. Annabel felt nervous and excited all at once. Her parents were coming to watch. Most importantly, Nana would be there, sitting in the front row. Annabel waited in the wings, listening to the auditorium filling up.

She couldn't believe she was going to dance in front of all these people.

The Magic Dancing Shoes

"Hurry up, Annabel," called Miss Carr, interrupting her thoughts. "It's time to finish getting ready for the show."

Annabel rushed off to the dressing room to find her magic dancing shoes. But when she got there the shoes were gone! What on earth would she do? How would she ever dance as well as she had with the magic shoes?

Annabel felt tears welling up in her eyes. There was no way she could do the show now! How would she explain herself?

As she sat all alone, wondering what to do, Annabel suddenly felt the tiniest tap on her shoulder. Then there was a little whisper in her ear. "It's the big show, Annabel! Why are you sitting here crying?"

She rubbed her eyes and looked up to see the fairy ballerina spinning excitedly. "I've been watching you, Annabel, and you really are an amazing dancer." she said. "But my magic shoes are gone!" cried Annabel. "I can't dance without them."

The fairy looked over at her and smiled. "The shoes weren't really magic, Annabel!" she said. "The dancing was inside you all along. All you have to do is believe in yourself, and you will find that your heart knows every step." Annabel was shocked. Had it really been her dancing all this time, and not the shoes? Maybe she could do the show after all.

Annabel hurried to find Miss Carr, and together they went to find a spare pair of dancing shoes in the store wardrobe. Annabel put them on and made her way nervously to the stage. She stood behind the great big curtain, closed her eyes and breathed in deeply. The curtain rose slowly, and the music began.

From then on, the evening turned into a blur of spinning, jumping and swirling light and sound. Annabel was lost in the music and dancing.

When the curtain finally came down, Annabel was in a daze. She got changed and went to meet her parents and grandparents at the stage door. Everyone told her how amazing she had been.

"I've never seen you dance better, Annabel," said Nana, giving her a hug. "I'm so proud of you." Then she took her hand and whispered in her ear, "Don't worry, the fairy told me what happened. We'll get you a new pair of dancing shoes for those magic feet of yours!"

Annabel could only stare in amazement as her grandmother put a finger to her lips. "And if you keep it a secret," she whispered, "I'll even teach you some new steps!"

Chicken Little

Chicken Little was wandering through the woods one day when PLOP, something small and hard fell onto her head. "Ouch," said Chicken Little. "That felt like the sky was falling." But the sky was not falling. What Chicken Little had felt was an acorn falling from a tree, although she didn't know that.

On through the woods went Chicken Little when PLOP, something else fell on her head. "Ouch," she cried. "That really, really felt like the sky was falling." But of course, it was another acorn falling from a tree, although Chicken Little didn't know that.

She kept on walking when PLOP! PLOP! PLOP! Three acorns fell on her head all at once. "Help!" yelled Chicken Little. "The sky really is falling!"

Chicken Little

As she was rushing along, she bumped into Henny Penny, who was out for a stroll.

"Help!" said Chicken Little to Henny Penny, "the sky is falling!"

"Where?" asked Henny Penny, looking around in shock.

"Right on my head," said Chicken Little. "We must go to tell the King."

So, Chicken Little and Henny Penny set out to tell the King.

On the way, they met Ducky Lucky, who was going to the pond.

"Help!" said Henny Penny to Ducky Lucky. "The sky is falling!"

"Where?" asked Ducky Lucky, looking around in shock.

"Right on Chicken Little's head," said Henny Penny. "We must go to tell the King."

So Chicken Little, Henny Penny and Ducky Lucky set out to tell the King.

On the way, they met Cocky Locky, who was going to the barnyard.

"Help!" said Ducky Lucky to Cocky Locky. "The sky is falling!"

"Where?" asked Cocky Locky, looking around in shock.

"Right on Chicken Little's head," said Ducky Lucky. "We must go to tell the King."

So Chicken Little, Henny Penny, Ducky Lucky and Cocky Locky set out to tell the king.

On the way, they met Goosey Lucy, who was going to the market.

"Help!" said Cocky Locky to Goosey Lucy. "The sky is falling!"

"Where?" asked Goosey Lucy, looking around in shock.

"Right on Chicken Little's head," said Cocky Locky. "We must go to tell the King."

So Chicken Little, Henny Penny, Ducky Lucky, Cocky Locky and Goosey Lucy set out to tell the King.

On the way, they met Turkey Lurkey, who was going to the meadow.

"Help!" said Goosey Lucy to Turkey Lurkey. "The sky is falling!"

"Where?" asked Turkey Lurkey, looking around in shock.

"Right on Chicken Little's head," said Goosey Lucy. "We must go to tell the King."

So Chicken Little, Henny Penny, Ducky Lucky, Cocky Locky, Goosey Lucy and Turkey Lurkey set out to tell the King.

Chicken Little

On the way, they met Foxy Loxy, who was going to his den.
"Help!" said Turkey Lurkey to Foxy Loxy. "The sky is falling!"
Where?" asked Foxy Loxy, looking around in shock.
"Right on Chicken Little's head," said Turkey Lurkey. "We must go tell the King."

But Foxy Loxy said that if the sky was falling, they would be safer waiting in his den until the danger was over. So Chicken Little, Henny Penny, Ducky Lucky, Cocky Locky, Goosey Lucy and Turkey Lurkey all followed Foxy Loxy into his den.

But of course it was not safe in the den and the danger was far from over, for Foxy Loxy gobbled up Chicken Little, Henny Penny, Ducky Lucky, Cocky Locky, Goosey Lucy and Turkey Lurkey. And the King never did find out that the sky was falling.

Snowfall the Unicorn

Far away, where the land meets the sea, there is a kingdom of great beauty. Mountains glisten with snowy tops and rivers cascade through green meadows filled with wild flowers. Neither man nor beast wants for anything.

But this was not always so. One year, springtime didn't bring the usual rains, and by summer the air was heavy with heat. It grew hotter and hotter, and the earth became cracked and parched. There was no harvest that year.

By late autumn, the King called together his most trusted advisors to discuss what could be done.

"My wise men, what suggestions do you have," asked the King, "for I fear my people will starve."

"A rain dance perhaps, your majesty? Maybe we have upset the gods," answered one advisor. The dancer was summoned, but no rains came.

The King once again called together his advisors.

"My wise men, what shall we do?" the king asked.

"Our food stocks are almost empty and my people are thirsty."

"Your majesty we could divert the great river from the north of the kingdom to provide water for everyone," suggested another.

So they journeyed to the north, but when they arrived the great river had dried up and disappeared.

43

Winter came, yet the terrible heat continued. Many of the people bade farewell to their homes and set off to other kingdoms in search of food and water.

On Christmas Eve, Princess Natasha, the King's youngest daughter, gazed sadly out of her bedroom window. In the moonlight she could see the dry and parched kingdom. Tears ran down her cheeks as she looked at the wretched landscape. "Will we ever see snow again?" she whispered to herself. "If only I could do something to save the kingdom. But what can a little girl like me do?"
Princess Natasha glanced up into the evening sky, where a lone star was twinkling. "Please, bring back the snow," she whispered.
The star twinkled even more brightly. Again she pleaded with the star, "Please, bring back the snow to our poor kingdom."
The star twinkled at her once more, and seemed to move. So Natasha put on her cloak and decided to follow it. She didn't know what else she could do.

The princess followed the bright star. She walked for hours through the dusty fields until she came to the dried-up forest. There, in the middle of a clearing, surrounded by withered trees, she found a unicorn bound with thick rope.

"You poor creature!" she cried, kneeling beside the beast. "Who could have done such a thing?"

The unicorn was very still, but when Natasha stroked its back it opened its eyes and looked at her sadly.

"Don't worry," said Princess Natasha. "I shall help you."

And she set about loosening the ropes, until eventually the unicorn was free.

Snowfall the Unicorn

As the magical creature rose from the ground something caught Natasha's eye:
a tiny white speck floated down from the sky and landed gently on her nose.
It was a snowflake!

Soon snowflakes were swirling all around them.
"Thank you, Princess Natasha," said the unicorn. "My name is Snowfall.
I control the seasons and bring the winter snow, but I was captured by a band
of hunters who tied me up. Unless I am free I have no magical powers."

The snow continued to fall all around them as the unicorn knelt before the
princess and offered his back to take her home. And as they rode through the forest
something magical happened. With each step they took the trees started to turn
green and the grass sprang from the earth once more. Soon the air was filled with
the sound of birdsong and forest creatures scurried among the growing hedgerows.

Snowfall the Unicorn

Finally they reached the King's castle, bringing with them the beautiful snow. It was the best Christmas gift anyone could ever ask for. When the King heard what had happened he begged Snowfall to stay at the palace so they could keep him safe. And so it came to be that the unicorn lived in the castle garden, and Natasha visited him every day.

Ever since that time, the long summer days are once again filled with bright sunshine, and when winter comes the land is always covered in a blanket of pure white snow. And every Christmas the people look up at the stars twinkling above them, and it reminds them of the terrible year when the unicorn was captured. And they give thanks to the beautiful creature who once again roams free.

Snow White & Rose Red

Once upon a time, a poor widow lived with her two daughters. The girls were called Snow White and Rose Red. They were named after two rose trees that grew in front of their cottage – one red, and one white. They were very sweet and kind girls.

The two girls were very happy. When they weren't busy helping their mother, they played in the forest. The animals watched over them and always made sure they were safe. If they ever got lost, a kind bird or deer would lead them back to their cottage. On warm summer nights, they sometimes slept outside, beneath the moon. On cold winter nights, they warmed themselves beside the fire.

One cold winter's evening, they were sitting beside the fire when there was a knock at the door. Rose Red ran to pull it open.

"Aaaaahhhh!" she screamed. She was face to face with a big, brown bear.

"Do not be afraid. I won't hurt you," said the bear in a surprisingly gentle voice.

"May I come in to warm myself beside your fire?"

"Please do, you poor bear!" said the widow.

And she welcomed him in.

48

At first, Snow White and Rose Red were afraid of the big, brown bear. Then, bit by bit, they became used to him. Before long, they were playing with him and having lots of fun.

For the rest of the winter, the bear was like one of the family. He slept beside the fire each night, and returned to the forest each day.

When spring arrived, the bear told the girls he had to go away. "I must guard my treasure from the wicked dwarfs who come out of their holes in the spring," he explained.

Later that day, Snow White and Rose Red were collecting firewood when they saw something dancing around a fallen tree. It was a angry-looking dwarf with a long, black beard. His beard was trapped beneath the tree.
"What are you staring at?" he yelled at the girls. "Why don't you help?"

The girls pulled and pulled, but they could not free the dwarf.
"You useless brats," snarled the dwarf. "I could die before you get me out of here!"
"Don't worry," said Snow White. "I will help you."

Then she pulled her scissors out of her pocket and snipped his beard.
As soon as the dwarf was free, he grabbed a bag of gold from among the tree's roots and turned his back on the girls.
"Nasty girl, cutting off my fine beard," he hissed. And then he was gone.

Shortly afterwards, Snow White and Rose Red were walking by the brook when they saw the dwarf again. A big fish had caught hold of his beard and was pulling him into the water. The two girls caught hold of the dwarf and tried to pull him free. But it was no use. The fish was just too strong. Not knowing what else to do, Snow White pulled out her scissors and cut the beard.

"You toadstool!" screamed the dwarf once he was free. "Do you want to ruin all of my beautiful beard?" Then, without another word, he dragged a sack of pearls out of the reeds and disappeared.

A few days later, Snow White and Rose Red were walking to town when they heard someone scream. They ran towards the noise and saw that a huge eagle had grabbed the bad-tempered dwarf.
"Quick," said Rose Red. And each girl grabbed one of the dwarf's legs. They pulled and pulled until the eagle finally let go.

Snow White & Rose Red

The dwarf jumped to his feet and grabbed a
bag of jewels.
"You clumsy creatures!" he snarled.
"Couldn't you have been more careful?
Look, my lovely coat is all torn."
He glared at the girls with fiery red eyes, and
then disappeared down a hole.

By now the girls were so used to the
ungrateful dwarf's bad manners that they
continued to town without giving him a
further thought.

Later that evening, the girls were returning
home when they saw something sparkling in
the moonlight. The dwarf was pulling sacks
of treasure out of a hole and spreading it out
on the grass. It looked so lovely that the girls
stopped to stare.

"What are you staring at?" screamed the
dwarf in a rage.

He didn't stop shouting at them until there was a loud growl and a brown bear leaped out of the forest.

The dwarf was so scared that he didn't move an inch.

"D...d...dear Mr. Bear," he spluttered. "Don't hurt me. I'm just a skinny little dwarf. I wouldn't make much of a meal. Eat those girls instead. They are plump and juicy."

The bear paid no attention to his words. He sprung forward and cuffed the dwarf with a powerful paw. The dwarf gave a yell and fell to the ground.

Meanwhile, the two girls had run away to hide.

"Come back, Snow White and Rose Red," called the bear in a gentle voice. "Don't be afraid. I won't hurt you."

It was their old friend, the bear.

Snow White and Rose Red ran to hug him. And when they did, the most surprising thing happened. His bearskin fell away to reveal a handsome young man, dressed from head to foot in gold.

"I am Prince Levi," he said. "That wicked dwarf stole my treasure and turned me into a bear. I was doomed to live as a bear for as long as he lived."

Snow White & Rose Red

As Snow White gazed into the prince's sea-blue eyes, her heart began to pound. She was falling in love. Luckily, Prince Levi felt exactly the same.

Not long afterwards, there was a huge wedding. Snow White married Prince Levi and Rose Red married his brother, Prince Sebastian. The girls and their mother moved to the castle, and they all shared the treasure. But none of the treasure was as dear to them as the two rose trees that grew outside the castle gates – one red and one white.

The Missing Pony

Gemma was stuck on the second level of her computer game. "You're not still playing that, are you?" said her mother, coming into her bedroom. "It's such a lovely day out. Why don't you get some fresh air instead?"

Gemma groaned. Her mother was always nagging her to get some fresh air, but the truth was she hated going out lately because that meant walking past the empty field by the side of the house.

The field hadn't always been empty. Two months ago it had been home to Merry, a beautiful little roan pony, but a horse thief had come along one winter's night, and now the pony was gone.

Tears stung Gemma's eyes, but she refused to cry any more. She looked back at the computer screen; try as she might, she just couldn't get onto the next level, so a break might not be such a bad thing. She went down the stairs and gave a soft whistle.

In a flash of brown and white, her little terrier, Benji, came charging at her, wagging his tail furiously. A walk might cheer her up. Gemma and Benji headed to the place they always went: a smooth flat rock at the top of the hill that overlooked the town. There was hardly ever anyone around at this time of day, so she could let Benji run around freely and let her thoughts drift. And today, as usual, her thoughts drifted to Merry. She missed her little pony so much. She missed riding her and nuzzling her neck.

The Missing Pony

Gemma was lost in her thoughts when the sound of Benji yapping and tearing off down the opposite side of the hill made her snap out of it. In the distance Gemma could make out a figure coming from the woods, heading towards her with Benji jumping around her feet. Benji, who didn't like strangers, never behaved this way, especially since Merry had been stolen.

As the figure got closer she saw the girl scoop the little dog into her arms. She was worried until she recognized who it was – Mary Donnolly, a girl she knew a little from school.

Although Gemma and Mary were in the same class, the girls didn't know each
other very well at all. Gemma's friends all thought that Mary was a bit strange and
avoided her. It was true that Mary was a little different from the other girls. She wore
slightly odd clothes, and she was always on her own, reading books about plants
and animals. When you did speak to her she didn't talk about ordinary things like
phones or downloads, and Gemma guessed she was the sort of person who
liked to be alone. Some of the other girls joked that Mary could do magic, but
Gemma thought that was mean, so she always gave her a smile when they passed
in the corridor.

The Missing Pony

As she walked up the hill with the runaway terrier tucked under her arm, Mary recognized Gemma as one of the popular girls at school. She was pretty, wore trendy clothes, and had a lot of friends who were also popular. But unlike the other girls, who nudged each other and whispered as Mary walked past, Gemma had always seemed kind. As the classmates drew closer they smiled shyly, but when Mary handed over the little dog she wondered why she saw such sadness in Gemma's eyes. "What's wrong?" she asked. "You look like you're missing something."

Gemma was startled by Mary's keen observation. "I'm thinking about my missing pony," she replied without thinking. Mary gave an understanding nod, but Gemma blushed. Why had she shared her secret with someone she hardly knew? "Bye for now," she smiled awkwardly, turning to leave.
"See you at school."

As Mary headed down the hill she was lost in thought. She could not forget the sadness in Gemma's eyes. "I must do my best to help her," she whispered. When she got home, Mary went straight to her herb garden and picked a sprig of sweet-smelling rosemary.

The Missing Pony

"For remembrance," she smiled, as she put it in her basket. Next she picked lucky lavender, and a handful of dandelions puffballs. As she did this Mary thought about the girls at school, and how surprised they'd be to know that some of the things they whispered about her were true – sort of. She wasn't magic, of course. But she was different; she had a special gift. She used natural remedies to cure sick animals. And there was something else, too, which she couldn't quite explain. When she made wishes, they sometimes came true. She knew the others at school found her odd and shy, and this made her unpopular. But she didn't know how to change things. And no amount of wishing for friends of her own seemed to help. Her wishes only seemed to work for others . . .

That evening, Mary wove the rosemary and lavender into a ring around a pot, and put the dandelions in the middle. Then she sat down to think about Gemma and her lost pony. Mary held up the pot in the moonlight and gently blew.
The dandelion seeds drifted away on the cool night breeze as Mary made a wish.

In a nearby valley a little roan pony was falling asleep in her stall when the cool night breeze stirred her. She sniffed and began to wake up. Her new owners worked her so hard that she was always so tired these days, but suddenly she felt she could shake off her exhaustion. She was restless.

She started to paw the floor, then she started to kick the door. Finally she used her hind legs to smash the door off its hinges, and she ran out into the night. There was somewhere else she was supposed to be; she remembered that now, and finally she was going home.

Gemma never knew how her beloved Merry came to be whinnying under her bedroom window that night. She never found out where she had been or who had taken her. But she didn't really care. She only cared that she was home and her heartache was over.

The Missing Pony

But there was one thing about the day her pony came home that nagged at her. When she had locked eyes with strange little Mary Donnolly on the hillside she had seen compassion and wisdom, but also something else; loneliness.

Gemma nuzzled Merry's soft, velvety nose and hugged her silky, smooth neck, then leaped up onto her newly saddled back. As they headed off towards the woods, Gemma urged Merry into a trot and called for Benji to catch up.
"Come on boy," she called to the little dog.
"We're off to make a new friend."

The Bee Wing Ball Gown

Why aren't you drawing Australia?" The teacher's voice made Paula jump. "Even fashion designers must learn geography!"

"Sorry, Mrs. Frazer."

"Let's see!" giggled Paula's best friend, Yasmin. Paula looked around. Mrs. Frazer was at the front of the classroom talking to Josie, the new girl in their class. Paula showed Yasmin her sketch of a wide hat with a feathery plume bending down from the brim. "You're so good at drawing!" said Yasmin.

Yasmin's mother walked the girls home from school that afternoon. She strode ahead with Yasmin's baby brother, Adam, in his buggy, reading the school newsletter as she walked.

"Have you seen this?" she called, waving the newsletter in the air.

"'This year's play is *Cinderella*,'" she read. "'Come and paint scenery or make up a song. Or take part in our competition to design *Cinderella's* ball gown. The winning design will become a real dress for the play!'"

Yasmin and Paula hugged each other.

"I've got loads of ideas," said Paula, eyes shining.

"And you can talk about them tomorrow," laughed Yasmin's mother. "Now let's get home."

The Bee Wing Ball Gown

At school the next morning, Paula fidgeted while the nursery-school children told a story about a troll, accompanied by Mrs. Spender's music class. At last it was time for Mrs. Frazer to read the school news.

"There's a meeting next Wednesday for all *Cinderella* actors and scenery makers. And the ball gown competition is now open for entries. We can only accept entries if you work with a partner."

"Yippee!" whispered Yasmin.

"And the teachers will choose the partners," Mrs. Frazer continued.

There were lots of questions, but Paula didn't hear them. There was no chance that Mrs. Frazer would let her work with Yasmin. Yasmin grabbed Paula's hand.

"Maybe we can swap partners," she whispered.

After lunch, Mrs. Frazer announced the pairs.

"Yasmin," said Mrs. Frazer. "You're with Maya."

Yasmin grinned. Maya loved drawing. She once won a competition for her artwork, so she would be a great help.

"And Paula . . . " Mrs. Frazer consulted her list. "You're with Josie."

Josie? The new girl who never wore dresses and only liked bugs? Paula tried to smile at Josie, but Josie was staring at her desk. Paula turned to Yasmin, but her best friend was chatting excitedly to Maya. Suddenly Paula felt very alone.

That evening, Paula pulled her old fairy tale books from her shelf. She copied some gowns, carefully adding collars and bows, trying out different shades and patterns. She spread the drawings across the kitchen table.

"Very impressive," said Dad. "They could win any competition."

"I can't use them," Paula complained. "My partner's Josie and she's bound not to like anything this girly."

"Well," soothed Dad, sitting down next to her, "no point starting over if you already have something to work with."

"You're right!" Paula added a pink cloak with a furry hem to a ruffled gown.

"Josie won't mind if I do most of the work. Then she won't have to do something she hates."

At break the next morning, Paula spotted Josie crouched by a bush. Paula crouched down beside her.

"Ssh," said Josie. "See that ladybug? I don't want to disturb it."

Paula pulled out her drawings.

"Josie, I know you're not really into fashion design. These are for the competition. You pick one and I can enter it for both of us." The ladybug clambered onto a leaf and flew away. Josie looked through the pictures and handed them back. Silence.

"Do you like them?" asked Paula nervously. Josie shook her head.

"Why?" Paula demanded.

"They're just . . . well . . . boring," said Josie quietly.

Paula's eyes prickled. She stuffed the pictures back in her bag, not caring if they wrinkled or tore. "Well, you're boring too! All you're interested in is bugs!"

The Bee Wing Ball Gown

Just after supper, Paula's doorbell rang and she heard the mumble of voices.
"Paula?" called her mother.

The woman at the door was tall, with curly hair and a friendly smile.
"I'm Josie's mother," she said. "I heard you two had an argument. Would you like to come over for an hour or so?"

Paula hesitated.
"You could still win that competition," Paula's mother reminded her.

Josie lived on the sixth floor of a tall building on a busy street. The door opened and Paula stepped into a room that smelled of hot sugar.
"We're trying out a new popcorn machine," said Josie. "We can have some later."

Josie pushed open a door. "This is my bedroom."

Paula walked in and immediately jumped out again. A massive spider hung on the wall opposite.

"It's only a poster," laughed Josie. "And most spiders are harmless."

"Don't they bite?"

"Not all," said Josie. "But they do have forty-eight knees."

Paula stared at the picture.

"And worms have five hearts," Josie told her. "But no noses at all."

When Josie's mum brought in the popcorn, the girls were poring over a drawing book.

"Do you copy these from pictures?" Paula was asking.

"Sometimes I watch the insects in the park," said Josie. "And my cousin's got a wormery. You can see the worms moving inside."

Paula stroked a drawing of a bee's wing.

"It's like lace,'" she said. "I can't believe you can draw like this."

"Well I only copy the animals I'm interested in, I guess they're not bad pictures," replied Josie, shyly.

69

The final day of the competition arrived. Mrs. Frazer cleared a board to show off the entries. Paula and Josie examined the display. There were eighteen ball gowns. Many had long puffy skirts. Some were decorated with cloaks, others with jewel-encrusted belts. Yasmin's and Maya's was a sweeping gown of gold cloth with scarlet shoes and a sparkly headband.

Paula and Josie's design was nothing like the others. It had red shoes with black spots, leggings as green as a cricket and a shiny, beetle-black top. A floor-length lacy wing fell from each shoulder. The outfit was completed by a pink hat.

"Cinderella's got a worm on her head!" laughed a little boy.
Mrs. Frazer arrived with a man that the children had never seen before.
"Mr. Lee is helping me judge," she said. "He designs costumes for films and plays."
Excitement rippled through the hall. Paula and Josie held hands tightly. So did Yasmin and Maya. The judges examined every picture, whispered together and wrote some notes. Finally, Mr. Lee stepped forward.

"We have a winner," he said. The girls held their breath.
"We loved them all." He paused. "But the winner is . . . Yasmin and Maya."

Yasmin and Maya grinned as everybody clapped. Josie turned to Paula.
"I bet you wish Yasmin was your partner," she said.
"No!" Paula was surprised. "I'm really glad we've become friends."

"Josie? Paula?" Mrs. Frazer beckoned. Mr. Lee was holding their picture.
"This is very different," he said. "Not quite right for Cinderella. But it's perfect for the Carnival Queen Bee leading our procession this year. Can we use it?"
"Yes, please," gasped the girls.
"And you two can ride on the Carnival float," said Mrs. Frazer.

Josie and Paula looked at each other.
"Thank you," said Josie. Paula grinned and clasped Josie's hand. They might not have won the school competition but they were to be in the carnival parade!
It couldn't be a better prize!

The Six Swans

Once upon a time, there lived a King who had one daughter and six sons. The King loved his children very much, for his wife had died many years earlier and they were the only relations he had left in the world.

One day, the King went hunting. He rode deeper and deeper into the woods following a stag, until all at once he realized he was lost. Each way he turned the paths looked the same. He grew more and more worried until suddenly he spotted an old woman sitting on a tree trunk.
"Excuse me," said the King politely. "Could you show me the way out of the woods so I can find my way home?"

The woman saw his royal robes and realized at once that he was a King.
"I will show you on one condition," she answered slyly. "You must marry my beautiful daughter and take her to be Queen of your land."
"And what if I do not care to take the hand of your daughter?" asked the King.
"Then I will leave you alone for the wild animals to hunt!" she replied.

The King was worried about his children, so he was forced to agree.

The next day the King kept his word and married the woman's daughter.
But he saw that she would not be a kind stepmother to his children, so he asked his servants to hide his family in a castle, deep in the oak forest.

Every morning, before the sun rose, the King left his wife sleeping and went to visit his children. Then he crept back to his bed before his wife noticed.
One day, however, his wife woke early and noticed that he was gone. The same thing happened the next morning. She became suspicious and decided to follow him.

The Six Swans

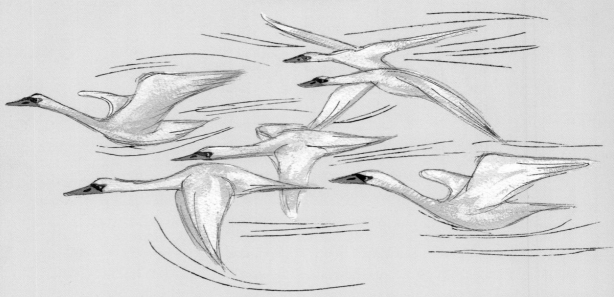

On seeing that he had seven children hiding in a castle, the Queen became very angry. She took a ball of magic string she had been given by her mother and, using a spell she had learned from her, turned the string into magic shirts made of pure white silk.

The next time the King went out hunting, the evil Queen hurried to the castle in the oak forest. Thinking it was their father arriving, the six boys rushed outside to greet him. Immediately, the Queen threw the magic shirts over them. At once, the six boys were turned into six white swans, and all flew away.

When the King went to visit his children the next morning, only his daughter remained. He was heartbroken when she told him what had happened.
"You must stay here until I can find a new, safe place to hide you," he told her.

That night, as the winds howled, the daughter was sure she heard her brothers calling in the forest, so she left the castle to look for them. All night she searched and searched, until she could go no further.

At last she spotted a hut.
"Maybe I can shelter here," she thought, opening the door. Inside she saw six beds. She longed to lie down, but she was worried that the owners might return, so she hid herself under one and closed her eyes to sleep.

The Six Swans

The girl was woken by the sound of beating wings. Opening her eyes, she was amazed to see six swans land on the beds. As each landed, its feathers fell off, revealing her six handsome young brothers.

"My brothers!" she cried, climbing out from under the bed.

They were overjoyed to see each her, and they all hugged tightly. But the brothers were worried, too.

"You must not stay here," they told her. "This hut isn't safe. We cannot protect you, for we are only human for a few moments each day before we turn back into swans."

"There must be something I can do to help?" said their sister.

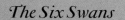

"There is," replied her oldest brother, "but it will not be easy. For six years you must not speak or laugh. And in your solitude you must sew six shirts made of the tiniest flower petals."

Before another word could be spoken, the six brothers turned back into swans and flew away. At once, their sister set off in search of the tiniest flowers she could find. Her search took her to another kingdom, where a carpet of the daintiest flowers she had ever seen grew on the forest floor. There she sat down and began to sew.

The next day the King of the land passed by.
"What are you sewing with my prettiest flowers?" he questioned. But the girl could not speak, of course, so she just kept on sewing.

The King was enchanted by this beautiful silent girl who sewed so diligently. He visited her every day, and every day he fell a little more in love with her.

Before the summer was over, he had persuaded her to marry him, even though she had never spoken a word.

The King's mother did not like this new, silent girl. So she decided upon a plan to get rid of her. After the girl gave birth to the King's first child, the mother stole the baby and spread lies that the girl had given it away. The young Queen's heart was broken, but she could not speak to say what had happened, so she just carried on sewing. The King, who loved his wife, refused to believe the lies.

When the young Queen had another child and it too went missing, the evil mother demanded that her son take action. But the King still loved his wife dearly, and knew in his heart that she would never give away their child.

When the third child went missing, however, the King began to doubt his heart. "My wife wants to do nothing more than sew all day long, every day," he thought. "Perhaps my mother is right about her."

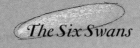

"Surely, if your wife is not guilty then she would tell you so," said the evil mother. Of course, the young Queen could not speak the truth, or any other words, so the King mistrusted his heart and decided she should be punished.

The next day was the day of the Queen's judgment. But it was also the end of the Queen's six years of silence. All through the night she sewed and sewed. By morning she had finished the six shirts, except for the last sleeve of one.

As the Queen stood before the King, her fate to be decided, the air was filled with the noise of beating wings and the trumpeting of swans. At once, the Queen threw the petal shirts over the swans' heads and the spell was finally broken. Before her stood her six brothers, one with a wing of a swan as an arm, for it was that shirt she had not finished in time.

"At last I can speak!" she cried. When the King learned what his mother had done, he sent her away forever. The six brothers took it upon themselves to find their missing nieces and nephews the mother had hidden, and it was to great celebration that they returned home with the missing children. The King was so grateful he invited his wife's brothers to live with them, for their father had passed away in the six years gone.

And so it was that the King, Queen, their children and the six brothers all lived together in happiness for the rest of their lives.

The Six Swans

The Butterfly Garden

Lottie, Sam and Michelle were the best of friends. One day, just before school ended for the summer, they were wandering home along the lane that led to their road, when all at once they stopped. Dancing in front of them was the most beautiful butterfly they had ever seen.

"It's so pretty!" whispered Sam. "I wish I was a butterfly."

Another butterfly appeared, then another, and another. There were butterflies everywhere. The three girls watched, enchanted, as the gentle creatures swirled around them then fluttered back up the lane.

"Let's follow them!" cried Lottie, grabbing her friends' hands.

The girls followed the fluttering trail through the park and into the town, until they came to a door in a wall behind the bus stop. The door was slightly ajar.

"Do you think we should follow them?" whispered Michelle.

"Absolutely!" cried Lottie. She grabbed hold of her friends once again and pulled them through the doorway before they could protest.

The girls stepped out into a sun-drenched public garden.

"Oh!" gasped Sam. "It's beautiful!"

The velvety lawn was divided by archways dripping with flowers. Right in the middle was a pond with a fountain. Everywhere the girls looked, there were butterflies and other creatures. Birds sang and dragonflies hummed as the girls wandered along the walkways, breathing in the scent of a thousand flowers.

The Butterfly Garden

It was only when they reached the fountain that Lottie found her voice.
"I don't think I've ever been anywhere as pretty as this. I can't believe it was just sitting here in the middle of town all this time."

The girls sat in the garden and looked around for a long time, until their tummies began to rumble and they remembered it was nearly time for supper. Only then did they reluctantly go home.

Lottie, Sam and Michelle visited the garden almost every day that summer. They had picnics, played games, and chatted while watching the butterflies dance around. It was their secret.

One Sunday, towards the end of the summer, Sam was having lunch with her family when something in the conversation made her sit up and pay attention. Sam's dad was talking about a new shopping mall that was going to be built in the middle of town. As she listened, it slowly dawned on Sam where they were planning to build it. They were going to build it right on top of the garden. The news upset Sam so much, she could barely finish her lunch. Afterwards she ran upstairs to her room and burst into tears. Their beautiful secret garden was going to be destroyed. It was more than she could bear.

The Butterfly Garden

Later that day Sam met her friends at the garden as usual, and told them the terrible news.

"We've got to do something!" cried Lottie. "This must be why the butterflies led us here, so that we could save their garden!"

"But what can we do?" asked Michelle. "Who will listen to us?"

Lottie was adamant. "We have to try. We can't let it be destroyed."

All afternoon, the girls discussed ways to save the garden. They felt sure that if others knew how wonderful it was, then maybe they could convince the town council to save it.

"I know," said Lottie. "Why don't we organize a party at the garden?"

"Great idea!" the others agreed. "Then everyone can see how special it is."

The girls spent the rest of the week making invitations, which they mailed to everyone they could think of: friends, parents, teachers – even the mayor.

When the day of the party arrived, the girls spent the whole morning preparing food and drinks for their guests. They borrowed chairs and tables and arranged them around the garden.

Finally they hung banners from the trees that said, "Save the Butterfly Garden!"

As the guests arrived, the three friends showed them around, and told them about the shopping mall. "We must save the garden!" they explained. "It doesn't just belong to the town. It belongs to all the creatures that live here too."

Everybody who saw the garden agreed that it had to be saved, and they all signed a petition. Soon the girls had over one hundred signatures. At the end of the afternoon, the girls approached the mayor, who was sitting admiring the fountain.

"Excuse me," said Lottie nervously. "We'd like to present you with our petition to save this garden."

"Thank you," said the mayor kindly, "but I'm afraid that the plans have already been approved. I'm sorry, but the decision is out of my hands at this stage. So, girls, unless you can come up with a miracle, this wonderful garden will be knocked down." And with a sad smile the mayor left.

The girls were devastated. They sat in a corner, unable to believe that they had failed, even with all the signatures and hard work they had put in.

"Never mind," consoled Sam's father. "Maybe there's something else you can do to save the garden. But right now we need to tidy up this mess."

The three girls started to clear up all the leftovers.

The Butterfly Garden

"It's not fair," sighed Michelle, gazing at a purple butterfly, sitting on the rim of a cup she was holding. "Why are buildings more important than a beautiful butterfly like this?"

Lottie turned to look. A strange expression came over her face.

"Don't move, Michelle," she whispered. "Sam! Quick! Bring me my camera. I think that butterfly is a Cornhill Beauty. It's a very rare species. I saw one in my wildlife book the other day."

Sam and Michelle held their breath as Lottie held up the camera and fiddled with the lens. SNAP! She just managed to take a picture before the butterfly fluttered away.

"I think we might just have found our miracle," cried Lottie, grinning from ear to ear. "We can email this picture to the Science Museum. Cornhill Beauties are a protected species!"

The girls waited anxiously all the following day for a reply to their email.
"Maybe they didn't get it!" suggested Sam, after they had checked their in-box for the hundredth time that afternoon. "Let's send it again."
Suddenly, the computer went *ding*.

"We've got mail!" cried Lottie, clicking on her in-box. The three girls eagerly crowded around the computer screen.
"It's from the Science Museum," read Sam. "It *is* a Cornhill Beauty. The head zoologist wants to come and see the garden for himself. He says that if Cornhill Beauties really live there, it must be a protected habitat. The shopping mall will have to be built somewhere else. He is going to speak to the planning department at the town hall right away."

And that's exactly what happened. It wasn't long before the local newspapers were full of the story about Lottie, Michelle and Sam, and how they had saved the garden from demolition. The girls even received a letter from the mayor, thanking them for all their hard work.

The Butterfly Garden

"Our garden is going to be renamed," said Lottie, as she read the letter out loud. It's going to be called The Butterfly Garden."

Now the whole town enjoys The Butterfly Garden. But nobody loves it more than Lottie, Sam and Michelle. To this day, they hold a party there every summer to celebrate its rescue, and to remind everyone how just how special it is.

The Little Mermaid

Far beneath the clear blue waves, the Little Mermaid lived in her father's kingdom with her five sisters and her grandmother. She was the youngest of her sisters, and the loveliest of them all. Her beautiful voice carried far across the water as she sang happily to herself.

More than anything else, the Little Mermaid loved to listen to her grandmother as she told tales of the world above the sea. She was mesmerized by her grandmother's descriptions of human beings and their ships, of the birds that flew high in the sky and the busy towns by the seashore. But it would be some years before the Little Mermaid could discover these things for herself; for a mermaid had to be fifteen before she was allowed to rise to the surface to see these extraordinary sights.

One by one, as they reached their fifteenth birthday, the Little Mermaid's sisters made the journey to the world above the ocean and came back with wonderful stories of what they had seen. The Little Mermaid longed to see these things for herself and waited impatiently for her fifteenth birthday.

On the day she turned fifteen, she could barely contain her excitement as she held on to her sisters hands and they started to swim towards the surface.

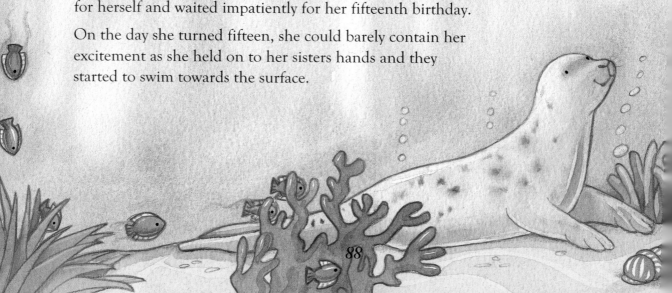

As her head popped above the waves for the first time, the Little Mermaid gasped – for the moon's rays glittered on the water and the clouds glowed green and blue. It was the most beautiful thing the Little Mermaid had ever seen.

Suddenly, the peaceful scene was shattered by a loud explosion. There before her was a ship, lit up by fireworks in the sky. Laughter drifted across the water.
On board the ship a party was under way to celebrate a young Prince's birthday. The Little Mermaid watched as the humans danced on the deck. She gazed at the handsome Prince and imagined herself twirling around in his arms.

As the celebrations went on, the calm seas gave way to waves. They were gentle at first, but the wind grew stronger and soon huge waves were crashing onto the boat's deck. With a terrifying groan, the deck split in two and the ship began to break up in the swirling waters.

The Little Mermaid

The Little Mermaid watched in horror as the handsome young Prince was thrown into the churning sea. At first he swam against the waves, but soon he grew tired and slipped beneath the surface. Down, down, down he sank.
"I must save him," cried the Little Mermaid. With a flick of her tail, she dived beneath the heaving waves and scooped up the young man in her arms.

The Prince was heavy and at times the Little Mermaid feared she would never reach the surface, but finally the waves parted and the Little Mermaid felt the wind on her cheeks once again. She held the Prince tightly in her arms and allowed the waves to carry them towards the shore. Just as the first rays of the sun peeped above the horizon, the Little Mermaid felt sand under her tail.

The little Mermaid stayed with the Prince on the beach for as long as she dared, singing to him softly. But as the sun's rays grew stronger, she knew that she had to return to the water.

The Little Mermaid

The Little Mermaid could not stop thinking about the handsome Prince. Every day she sat on the rocks in the bay to watch him walking in the palace gardens. At first this was enough, but after a while she longed to speak with him.

"But that will never happen," she sighed. "I'll never be human."

"You could be, if you wanted," said a voice next to her. The Little Mermaid turned to find herself face to face with a Sea Fairy. The Little Mermaid hesitated. Sea Fairies were always trouble! But then again, she did seem to know of a way that the Little Mermaid could be human.

Ignoring her doubts, the Little Mermaid followed the Sea Fairy.

"I have a potion that will change your tail into legs so you can walk with your Prince," cackled the Sea Fairy. "If you can make him fall in love with you before the sun sets on the second day, you will become human forever. If you fail, you will become a mermaid once more, but must serve me for all eternity!"

The Little Mermaid nodded her agreement as the Sea Fairy passed her a small bottle containing the powerful potion.

The Little Mermaid

The Little Mermaid swam slowly towards the surface with the potion bottle held tightly in her hand. Finally she reached the shore, and sat on the sandy beach below the palace on the cliff. With trembling hands, she uncorked the potion.
It smelled terrible!

Shutting her eyes, she put the bottle to her lips and quickly drank the liquid. Her throat burned and her eyes watered, but it was soon forgotten as the Little Mermaid saw her tail change before her very eyes into two pale legs. Very slowly, she stood up and took her first wobbly steps.

Meanwhile, at the palace, the Prince was gazing far out to sea, thinking about the mysterious girl who had rescued him.
"All I can remember is that she had a beautiful singing voice," he told his servant.
"If only I could find her. I long to hear her voice again."

The Little Mermaid

Just then, the Prince's servant spotted a bedraggled girl walking up the cliff path. "She must be a survivor from the shipwreck," cried the Prince. "Bring her into the palace and take care of her." He did not recognize the Little Mermaid.

The Little Mermaid was overjoyed to be invited into the palace – especially when she found herself sitting next to the handsome Prince at dinner. But her happiness was short-lived. For at the meal she heard something terrible.
A princess from the nearby kingdom was arriving the next day. The Prince's parents wanted him to marry her.

With a heavy heart, the Little Mermaid retired to her bed. It seemed that tomorrow she would have return to the sea to spend her days serving the Sea Fairy.

As dawn broke the next day, a fanfare announced the arrival of the Princess's ship. The Little Mermaid watched from her balcony as the sails grew larger on the horizon. The ship got nearer and the Prince prepared to sail out to meet his very special guest.
"Will you come with me?" he asked the Little Mermaid. "I would like you to meet her."

The Little Mermaid made her way down the palace steps and climbed aboard the boat. The boat skimmed across the water and soon it was alongside the Princess's ship. Seeing the Princess, the Little Mermaid was filled with dismay.

She was very beautiful. Her blond hair shone in the sunshine and her eyes sparkled as she gazed at the Prince. The Little Mermaid was certain she had lost her Prince forever!

The Little Mermaid

Celebrations lasted for the rest of the day, but the Little Mermaid could not join in. How could she celebrate, when her Prince was to marry another? Soon the sun would dip behind the horizon, and she must return to the sea to become a slave.

Suddenly the Little Mermaid heard a splash. She looked up, it was her sisters! "All is not lost," they told her, when they heard their sister's tale. "We heard the Prince's servant say his master longs to hear the voice of the girl who rescued him. You must sing, sing with all your heart!"

So, as the sun began to set, the Little Mermaid sang the song she had sung to the Prince on the beach. The haunting melody drifted across the water to where the Prince was. At once, he rushed over to the Little Mermaid and embraced her. "It was you who saved me," he cried, planting a kiss her on her cheek. "I have searched for you everywhere! I will never let you go again!"
Just at that moment, the sun dipped behind the horizon. The spell was broken and the Little Mermaid's wish had come true – she would be human forever and stay with her handsome Prince!

96